Raintree is an imprint of Capstone Global Library Limited, a company incorporated in England
and Wales having its registered office at 7 Pilgrim Street, London, EC4V 6LB – Registered
company number: 6695582

www.raintree.co.uk
myorders@raintree.co.uk

Contributing artists: Dario Brizuela
Designed by Hilary Wacholz

Printed and bound in India

ISBN 978 1 4747 7583 0

22 21 20 19 18
10 9 8 7 6 5 4 3 2 1

LEX LUTHOR™

DC SUPER-VILLAINS

AN ORIGIN STORY

WRITTEN BY
IVAN COHEN

ILLUSTRATED BY
LUCIANO VECCHIO

SUPERMAN CREATED BY
JERRY SIEGEL AND JOE SHUSTER
BY SPECIAL ARRANGEMENT WITH
THE JERRY SIEGEL FAMILY

Far from Metropolis, a young man tries a new experiment inside a small lab. The man is close to making an amazing discovery: the secret of life.

"I will be the most famous scientist ever!" he says proudly.

The young man mixes two dangerous chemicals together.

BOOM! The chemicals explode. They spill onto the floor and spark a fire.

"Help! Help me!" The man coughs and chokes on the thick smoke.

Suddenly, a red and blue streak appears in the sky above the lab.

"Superman!" the man shouts, spotting the super hero through a window.

Superman breathes deeply. He cools the air inside his lungs. Then he blows out the fire with one breath. *FWOOSH!*

"No!" the young man screams.

Superman's powerful breath sprays chemicals across the lab and onto the man. Thick clumps of red hair sizzle and fall from his head.

"Are you OK?" asks the hero.

"You destroyed my hair and my greatest discovery!" the young man shouts. "You will pay for this, Superman. Or my name isn't . . .
Lex Luthor!"

At that moment, Luthor decides to never fail again. He will become more powerful, more famous than any person alive. He will rule Metropolis and then take over the world.

"No one will stand in my way," says Luthor. "Not even Superman!"

After years of hard work, Luthor's dream begins to come true. He starts his own company, LexCorp, in Metropolis. The company builds skyscrapers, motorways, bridges, stadiums and more.

Soon, Metropolis becomes the most powerful city on Earth.

Luthor becomes one of
the world's richest and
most powerful people. He
enjoys being at the centre of
everything.

One day, Luthor invites
reporters to his newest building.
The reporters listen closely to
his speech.

Photographers snap pictures
of the powerful businessman.

Just then, Superman soars past the LexCorp building. The hero flies to help someone in danger.

The reporters look to the sky. They stop listening to Luthor.

The photographers snap pictures of the super hero instead.

"Blast it!" Lex shouts, waving his fist angrily. *I must get rid of Superman,* he thinks, *once and for all!*

At first, Luthor hires criminals to help bring down the Man of Steel. He pays villains like Livewire and Parasite to do his dirty work.

But time and time again, these villains fail.

Only one thing can stop Superman, Luthor thinks. *Another Superman!*

Luthor returns to the lab. With new, more powerful equipment, his experiments are a success. He grows new life from a single drop of Superman's blood.

He creates a new Superman!

"HAHAHA!" Luthor laughs.

But the experiment soon fails again. The Superman copy becomes twisted and strange and bizarre. The copy tries to be a hero, but everything he does turns out backwards.

"Me am Superman," says Bizarro. "Me save tree from cat!"

After Superman defeats Bizarro, Luthor worries that the real hero will come after him.

Luthor decides to use Superman's greatest weakness instead – a radioactive rock from Superman's home planet.

"Kryptonite!" Luthor says.

Luthor meets up with an injured criminal named John Corben. He gives the criminal a new robot body powered by the Kryptonite. In return, Corben promises to use his new powers to fight Superman.

KA-POW! The Metallo robot fights Superman, but even he is no match for the Man of Steel.

Luthor does not give up. He has a new plan.

"I am the greatest scientist alive," says Luthor. "I will take care of this Superman problem myself!"

Lex builds a special battle suit to fight Superman himself!

The suit's rocket boosters allow Luthor to fly. Force fields protect him from getting hurt. Kryptonite weapons give him incredible strength.

At last, Luthor is Superman's most powerful enemy!

KA-BOOM!

Luthor and Superman clash over downtown Metropolis. As they battle, the enemies crash and smash into Luthor's own buildings.

The battle suit's Kryptonite weapons weaken Superman.

"Ha!" Luthor laughs. Then he turns towards the onlookers and says, "I am the greatest scientist ever!"

Behind Luthor, Superman's strength quickly returns. "Try again, Luthor," says the super hero.

"Huh?" The villain gasps.

WHAM! Superman surprises the villain with a single, knockout punch.

Luthor coughs and chokes inside the smoking battle suit. "Help! Help me!" he cries.

Superman pulls the villain out of the suit to safety.

The police arrive and handcuff Luthor. Superman soars into the air.

"You haven't heard the last
of me!" Luthor shouts as
Superman soars over his new
home in prison.

Luthor will not stop until
Superman is defeated. He will
not stop until he's the most
powerful man in the world.

LexLuthor

REAL NAME: ALEXANDER LUTHOR
CRIMINAL NAME: LEX LUTHOR
ROLE: BUSINESSMAN/SUPER-VILLAIN
BASE: METROPOLIS

Brilliant scientist Lex Luthor was admired by people in Metropolis and around the world. But when Superman became even more famous and more loved, Luthor devoted himself to bringing Superman down and becoming the greatest criminal mind of all time!

Luthor's brain is his greatest weapon. He may have the highest IQ on Earth.

The battle suit's armour can protect Lex from most physical attacks.

Luthor's battle suit gives him super-strength.

Luthor is a master of physical combat.

The battle suit has wrist cannons that shoot energy blasts that can hurt even Superman.

Rocket boosters enable Luthor to fly for a near unlimited amount of time at great speed.

THE AUTHOR

IVAN COHEN is a former editor and media-development executive at DC Comics. As a writer, Cohen's recent credits include the *Green Lantern: The Animated Series* comic book, articles for *Time Out* magazine, and an episode of the Cartoon Network television series *Beware the Batman*. The co-producer of *Secret Origin: The Story of DC Comics*, Ivan was also a consultant on the PBS documentary *Superheroes: The Never-Ending Battle*.

THE ILLUSTRATOR

LUCIANO VECCHIO currently lives in Buenos Aires, Argentina. With experience in illustration, animation and comics, his works have been published in the US, Spain, UK, France and Argentina. His credits include Ben 10 (DC Comics), Cruel Thing (Norma), Unseen Tribe (Zuda Comics), Sentinels (Drumfish Productions) and several DC Super Heroes books for Raintree.

GLOSSARY

bizarre very unusual or odd

chemicals dangerous liquids or gases often used by scientists

defeat to win a victory over

destroyed to completely break or ruin

lab short for "laboratory", a place where scientists perform experiments

sizzle to make a hissing sound in or as if in burning or frying

villain a wicked person

DISCUSSION QUESTIONS

Write down your answers. Refer back to the story for help.

QUESTION 1.

Why do you think Luthor doesn't like Superman? Use examples from the story to explain your answer.

QUESTION 2.

If Lex Luthor wasn't a super-villain, do you think he could be a super hero? Why or why not?

QUESTION 3.

Do you think Luthor could ever defeat Superman? Explain your answer.

QUESTION 4.

What is your favourite illustration in this book? Explain how you made your decision.

READ THEM ALL!!

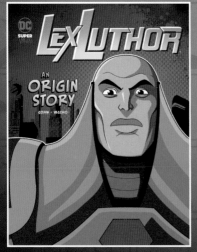